Gloria
A Diary

by
Joseph F. Girzone

Richelieu Court, Publishers
Albany, New York

Dedicated to all

the children in my life

young and old

Published

by

Richelieu Court Publications, Inc.

PO Box 13264

Albany, NY 12212-3264

Library of Congress Catalogue Card Number 82-80554

ISBN 0-911519-36-X

PREFACE

Teen-agers are not often given credit for deep thinking or for taking their lives seriously. Perhaps, it's because they shy away from serious discussions about topics that are important to them, because they are embarrassed or afraid they may be ridiculed.

The following pages, which are not entirely fictional, lay bare the inner life of a young girl, not unlike many young people of today. Her joys, her suffering, her problems, her friendships and love affairs, her groping for meaning to things are all very important to her.

Some things she can share with her friends, but the deepest and most important, she finds, she can share with no one; not her parents, certainly; not even her closest friends. Yet, she has to share her thoughts with someone, so in the dark quiet of her bedroom, where no strangers can intrude, she, like many teen-agers, finds God, and even though she is not particularly religious, shares with him all the experiences she knows she cannot share with anyone else.

I hope this book brings assurance and comfort to many young people, who so many times, have to find life's meaning all by themselves.

I also express deep appreciation to my friends and family members, as well as my many young friends for their help and guidance, which has been invaluable.

GROPING

GOD, I know I should probably address you as "Dear God," or "Good Lord," but I am not used to speaking that way and it seems "corny." I hope you understand. I've never prayed much before, except the way I was taught as a child, and it is hard for me to know what to say, but there are many things that confuse and trouble me that I have to talk to someone who understands. Somehow I know you understand, even if you don't talk back. You made me so you should understand me. I really can't talk to anyone else because my thoughts and feelings are so private, that I just can't share them with anyone else. They would think I'm odd. We don't talk about things like that when we get together or even when we're alone as friends. Yet these are the thoughts I think about most, and not being able to share them makes me feel so lonely. I just hope you understand me, God.

God, one of the things that bothers me terribly is you. When I was little I used to believe you were real. Now that I am older, I feel differently about things, and you are one of them. I think of you a lot, but I don't know whether you are real. So many of my friends don't believe in God. It seems the 'in' thing not to believe. In fact, some of the kids pray to the devil. I think that's sick. But, I still wonder whether you exist. When I'm happy I think you're real, but sometimes, when I get really 'down' and discouraged, I find it difficult to believe in you. And it doesn't help when I talk to you and you don't talk back. In fact, it doesn't even make sense. It would seem that if you really wanted people to believe you were real, the least you could do is talk to them.

Maybe you do talk to them in your own way, in a different way from what we're used to. Yesterday afternoon coming home from school, I was walking by myself. The autumn leaves are turning color, all kinds of colors. The sun was warm and it seemed to caress me. The birds were singing their simple songs, and a dog was barking in the distance. I looked up at the sky. It was cloudless, except for a single wisp that floated like a feather. I felt so good I could almost hear you talking to me. I knew you were real; I didn't have to hear your voice. I felt your presence in everything around me.

But, today everything went bad. My best friend said something terrible about me to one of my classmate, and rumors have spread all through the school. I made the mistake, God, of sharing a problem with my friend, because I had no one else to talk to, and she told her friends. I feel so betrayed. I'll never trust anyone again.

That wasn't all that happened. A little baby down the street that I baby-sit for died of leukemia this morning. Why did she die, God? It seems so meaningless, like a big mistake. It you knew she was going to die, why did you create her? It doesn't make sense. The baby's parents are all broken up and they are mad at you, God, and I don't blame them. They were good parents and they even went to church a lot.

It's times like these, God, when I find it difficult to believe that you are real, perhaps, because it's easier to believe that you are not real than to believe that you are cruel. I know I've never talked to you like this before. I hope you are not mad at me, but it's just the way I feel. I know this isn't the way people ordinarily pray, but I can't pray the other way anymore; I have too many things I have to talk to you about, and if you are real, I want to get to know you. So, if I seem irreverent or disrespectful, God, I hope you'll forgive me, because I want to be sincere and honest with you and what I say is just how I feel.

QUESTIONING

God, today I met a Jesus freak. He was weird. He said Jesus is all there is to life. He said Jesus follows me everyplace I go. He said Jesus is the great Judge who will one day herd us all together and make us account for everything we ever did wrong. That's spooky, God. It makes Jesus look like a big snoop who has nothing else to do all day but find things wrong with people and hold it against them forever. That's mental. If Jesus is like that, God, I don't want to have any part of him.

What is Jesus like, God? I was taught he was your son, and you sent him to earth to become a man. That seems almost like a punishment, God, to send Jesus from heaven to become one of us. That was horrible. He must have loved you a lot to obey you. I know I'd hate someone who made me become an ant, and that's what it must have been like for Jesus to become a man. Why did you do it, God? It just doesn't make sense. But, then, a lot of things you do don't make sense.

I thought a lot about Jesus today after I met that Jesus freak. I even got a book in the library about Jesus, but it was "corny" so I put it back. I wish I knew what Jesus was like, but there doesn't seem to be any way to find out. I tried to read the Bible once, but it was written in old-fashioned English, and was so boring I couldn't get into it. But, I would still like to know what Jesus was like. I don't know why; I guess he fascinates me and I'm curious about how he lived. When I think of Jesus, I think of a gentle man. It's hard to think of him as God or as a judge. I don't like the way they talk about him in church; they don't make him seem like much of a man, and, if I met him, I don't think I would like that kind of man.

Did Jesus always exist, even before he became a man? If he did, did he have a body? I guess he must have always existed if he was your son, God. And he couldn't have had a body before he was born. What was he then, just your image, God? I find you so difficult to understand. You're not really human, are you? But then, what are you? I can't even picture you. Are you like light? But light can't think and light can't love. Are you like my soul, my thoughts and my love? They are real but no one has ever seen them. It is so difficult talking to you, God, when I can't even imagine what you're like. And I'm not even sure you hear me. Oh, God, I'm so confused! I'm so tired, and it's late. Good night, God!

SCHOOL

God, I really liked school today. I don't know why it was different from any other day. Maybe it was this one teacher I got this year. He's really great, and so much different from the rest of the teachers, who are a bore. I love it in his class. He makes everything so interesting. He has soft, hazel eyes, and they seem to always twinkle. I know he likes me, because whenever he looks at me (and I sit right in front of him) he always smiles. I think about him a lot, even when I'm walking home from school. I like to think about him because I feel good inside. I think he's only a few years older than I am. I hope you don't mind that I like him so much, God, even though he's a priest.

I got 100 in my trigonometry test. I like math and science, but I did miserably in French. I can't stand it. Arlene is good in French. She's one of my friends. She's a lot of fun. This afternoon after basketball practice, we walked home together. She told me all about her family.

Her father's a doctor. He met her mother when he was an intern. She was a nurse at the same hospital. They only moved her last year, from Ohio. She misses her friends. Arlene's older sister goes to college. She has a brother and two sisters, but she can't stand her brother because he's so bossy.

I sort of envy Arlene, God. She got a beautiful figure. She's got a real nice personality, besides, and everybody likes her. Some of the boys tell me I'm pretty, but I don't think so. They say they wish they had my blonde hair and blue eyes, and all the boys talking about them the way they talk about me. But, I still don't think I'm pretty.

I got this record by the "Rolling Stones" today. It's just great. Some of my friends came over to my house to listen to it. We had a party and everybody had a swell time, except Chris; she was miserable. Her boyfriend broke up with her and she's really down. She gets in these real horrible moods, and I worry about her.

I even got my homework done today. I feel good about it, especially since I didn't do any all week, and my mother's been mad as hell. Well, I'm tired, God. Good night!

ALONE

Today was Sunday, God. The bells were ringing for church this morning, and I was tempted to go. Our family never goes, and I felt funny getting up and going alone, so I didn't go. None of my friends go. They don't like their minister. They say he's a 'fag.' I really don't see why people have to go to church anyway. What difference does it make? We can pray just as well at home as we can in church. Besides, a lot of people who go to church are 'phonies' anyway, like Jerry. He goes to church all the time. He even gives sermons in his church, and he tries to make out with all the married women in the neighborhood. I bet the minister doesn't know that.

And the man next door. He's a big lawyer in town. He's a trustee in our parish. My father was telling my mother how he and another lawyer swindled an old lady out of a fortune. They talked her into selling her land for practically nothing, knowing all along there was a gravel bed on her property. He evicted the old woman, and sold the land for three quarters of a million dollars. Everyone in the parish thinks he's great because he goes to church every Sunday, and teaches religion on Saturday morning.

I guess I'm not being very charitable. I really should go to church. There are a lot of people who go, people I really respect. I think they take their religion seriously, like Arlene's mother. She's beautiful. She spends two afternoons every week working with the retarded children in our school. And she does it for nothing. That really takes a lot of patience, God. I don't think I could do it.

I don't know why I don't like religion, God. Maybe it's because religion makes me feel so guilty, and takes all the fun out of life. You can't smoke; you can't drink; you can't 'make out' with boys. And you have to act so unreal. I like to be just what I am, and if I take religion seriously, I can't be me. I'd have to be a prude. And it would all be nothing but a big act anyway. It seems like a contradiction. You made us one way and put all these nice things in creation and then religion comes along and tells us we can't enjoy them, and it's a sin if we take pleasure in them.

I really can't believe you're that way, God. You're intelligent, and sometimes religion doesn't make sense. Maybe it's because ministers and priests don't really know you, or don't preach what they really think. They all seem to be so timid, and so disgustingly proper, like they're not human, like everybody else. I don't think you'd like religion either, God, if you were down here.

The ones that really get me though are the "born again" Christians. The act like they think they're the only ones who really love God. I think they're such phonies. There's one in my class. She's praising God all day long, and asks everybody if they're saved. I know she's not that religious. Last week she found out she was pregnant, and first thing went and had an abortion. I don't know whether that was right or wrong, God, but if she was really holy, I think she would have had the courage to have the baby.

I don't know what wound me up tonight, God. I guess I do have a lot of "hang ups" about religion, and feel very uncomfortable about it, especially on Sundays. Although, if Father Angelo, the priest who teaches in our school, were at our church, I think I'd go. He makes sense, and he really loves life, and he has such a happy attitude towards everything. When I think of him, I think of Jesus. But, I still like him a lot, God. Good night!

TROUBLE

Today was one of those days, God. It's a bad time of the month, and I felt miserable when I got up this morning. I was bitchy all day.

School wasn't all that bad, though. It was math day, and I like math. But, things didn't go well in Father Angelo's class. Maybe, I'm just being touchy, but he acted as if I didn't even exist. I felt terribly all day long. Maybe he has his own problems. He's got a tough job in our school. He was hired direct by the superintendent, because he has a reputation for being able to handle tough kids, and we have a lot of them. Ordinarily, priests don't teach in public schools, but I guess they made an exception in his case. I still wish I knew why he ignored me.

After lunch, the principal called a group of us into his office. He was mad as hell. He asked us if we were smoking "pot" in the john during lunch. We told him no, but he didn't believe us. I knew the girls in the john before us were smoking, but I wasn't going to tell him. He must have sensed I knew, because he dismissed the other girls and made me stay. He asked me if I smoked "pot", and I told him I tried it once or twice but I didn't like it, so I never smoked it again. In fact, I don't smoke anything. I think it's disgusting. Besides, I'm allergic to smoke. My eyes water and I have a hard time breathing when there's a lot of smoke in a room.

He asked me if I knew who was in the john before me. I told him no, but I felt guilty. He could see it in my face. I have a hard time lying. Then he sent me back to my classroom.

It turned out later that he found out who was smoking. The girls got me during the last period and were furious. They accused me of "ratting" on them.

The only fun part of the day was basketball after school. I made the team, and the coach told me I was really good. He asked me if I practiced much. I was a little embarrassed, but I told him I practiced everyday after school with the boys in the neighborhood. He grinned. I guess it did sound ambiguous. I tried to correct myself, and told him there was a hoop in the park near our house. He stilled laughed.

On the way home from school, we were crossing the street, and a car came screaming around the corner. It was Tommy and his new girlfriend. If I didn't jump back when I did, he would have run me over. Fortunately, he just nicked my knee. I didn't pay much attention to it then, God, but it hurts now, and I don't think I am going to be able to sleep. But, I'm tired of talking anyway, God. There's just one more thing, and I know I shouldn't ask, but I hope Father Angelo and I become real good friends.

WANDERING

I know it's been a long time since I talked to you last, God. Many things have happened since then. Thanksgiving is already past. We had a great time Thanksgiving Day. My mother's sister and my grandmother came from New Jersey. I went out with my friends early in the day and listened to the latest hits down at Gino's deli. We had our dinner late in the afternoon. It had been cool outside all day, and I was glad to get home. When I went inside I could feel my cheeks all flushed with the cold, and it was a big thrill to see the fire roaring in the fireplace. Everybody was in a good mood, and talking excitedly about everything that happened since Grandma's last visit.

The dinner was delicious. For weeks I look forward to the turkey dinner with all the gravy and sauces and desserts. It's the big feast of the year in our house. I love the feeling of coming into the warm house after being out in the cold, and smelling the turkey roasting in the over, and the pies baking. Looking back on the day, God, I don't think we thanked you for anything, even though we had such a good time. I don't even remember our family saying grace before the meal.

Other things happened since I talked to you last, God. Our basketball team has been doing great. The coach made me captain. I made eighteen points in the last game, and so far we've won eight out of the last nine games. This afternoon we played again, and I got ten baskets. We won thirty to fifteen. The last half of the game was difficult for me to play. My knee really hurt. I must have pulled a muscle.

The captain of the boys' basketball team invited me to the dance Saturday. I really like him. He's tall and has wavy hair, and thick eyebrows and real dark eyes. He must lift weights, because he's all muscles. Half the girls in my class have a "crush" on him, so I'm thrilled he asked me out. I can't wait until Saturday night. Today was a long day, God, and I'm really tired. Good night!

PARENTS

Oh, God! I feel miserable tonight. I had a big fight with my mother today. And it was about something so stupid. I promised Arlene I'd come over to her house after school. But, when I came home from school, my mother wanted me to go shopping for her. She could have gone herself. There was no way I could call Arlene, because her phone has been out of order. I tried to tell my mother, but she was in one of her moods, and wouldn't listen. So, we had a big argument. I told her to stop treating me like a child. After all, I'm almost seventeen. She didn't like what I said, and slapped me in the face. I was furious, God, and told her I hated her. Now I'm grounded for the week.

But, it didn't end there. She had to go and tell my father, when he came home from work. He took a fit and went into this big tirade about teen-agers. I tried to bite my tongue and not say anything, but he kept going on and on about how I never do anything I'm told, and how I've been independent ever since I was a kid, and he was tired of me doing just as I pleased.

I told him he should be glad I'm independent and do my own thinking, and when I defend myself, it's not being disrespectful. I'm just expressing my viewpoint, and if they didn't look at me as a little child, and treated me like a grown-up, we could have more intelligent conversations. Well, he didn't like that. He accused me of insinuating he was stupid, and stormed out of the house. My mother got mad all over again. I couldn't take anymore, God, so I just broke down and cried. I told her if nobody liked the way I am, everybody would be better off if I left home. I ran upstairs and slammed my door.

God, my parents are a big problem to me. I don't know what to do. I know I love them more than anyone else in my life, and I worry about them constantly. So many kids' parents are divorced. Sometimes, when my parents fight, and they sure have some hot ones, I get so nervous and afraid that they are going to get divorced. I think my whole world would fall apart if that ever happened. I feel so sorry for some of my friends whose parents are divorced. They seem to lose all their spirit and have all kinds of problems. Cindy used to be a straight A student before he father left home. Now she has no interest in studies, and just hangs around with a real tough crowd.

I think psychiatrists are stupid when they tell parents that they have to think of their own happiness when they're planning to get divorced, and that their kids shouldn't come into it. Kids didn't ask to be here, and if parents choose to have kids then they have to be responsible for them when they think about getting divorced. Kids suffer more than grown-ups. At least the adults are old enough to cope. Kids can't handle it, and they're all torn apart inside. Maybe kids should have a lawyer to take their side when parents have problems. They have rights, too.

Sometimes, God, I worry about my parents dying. I don't know what I'd do if anything ever happened to them. I really didn't mean it when I told my mother I hated her. I do love her so much. I guess I've never told her I love her. It's so hard to talk like that, especially to parents. I know I should try to be more patient with them. I'll make it up to Mom tomorrow. I don't have to worry about Dad; he'll be all right. He's probably over at one of his buddies' house now having a few drinks. Tomorrow he'll forget all about what happened tonight. I wish I could.

I think my mother is coming up the stairs.... Yes, it was her. We made up. I feel a lot better now. Good night, God!

MIKE

Mike and I had a great time last Saturday night, God. I forgot to talk to you since; I've been so busy. We went to the dance. It was really funny, God. Mike's not a dancer. When we got on the dance floor, he froze. He asked me what you're supposed to do next. I tried not to laugh, but he looked so pathetic. I told him just to follow me, and move the way I move. After a while he was having a good time. He's a lot of fun. We stayed until eleven o'clock, then the whole gang went to Gino's for pizza and coke.

Gino's is only two blocks from my house, so Mike and I walked home. When he held my hand, God, I got this nice feeling all over. About a block from our house, there's a big maple tree that hid us from the street light. I looked up at Mike and he looked at me. We both must have been thinking the same thing. He put his arms around me and held me tight. I looked up at him and wanted so much for him to kiss me. He seemed a little shy, and just put his face against mine and kissed my cheek. He told me that ever since school started he had wanted to take me out, but was afraid to ask. He told me he loved me and then his lips touched mine. I melted, God, and I really kissed him hard. We kissed for a long time. It was such a nice feeling and I didn't want it to end, but my jerky sister drove by with her boyfriend. They saw us and honked the horn, so we broke up and continued walking home.

I lay in bed a long time that night thinking of Mike. It was nice to be in love. I hope Mike really loves me and isn't just saying it.

The next day was Sunday. I slept late. I was really tired. Mike called in the afternoon and I talked to him for almost an hour. My sister and my brother wanted to use the phone, so they kept interrupting. There's more arguing in our house over the phone than over anything else. Everybody should have their own phone.

I thought of Mike the whole rest of the day, and couldn't wait to see him in school the next day. After supper, my mother asked me who Mike was. But, how do you explain about someone you like? All my mother could tell was that I liked him, and that was enough to press the panic button. I could tell another crisis was brewing, so I tried to keep calm. I tried to reassure her that it was nothing serious. In fact, I just met him. He's the captain of the basketball team, and he's on the honor roll. We probably won't go out much, because he's really busy. But, I do like him a lot.

She seems to like the part about him being busy. I could see she was more relaxed. She said she'd like to meet him sometime. Maybe he could come over for dinner next Sunday. It sounded like a good idea, so the conversation ended on a pleasant note for a change. I guess I can talk to my mother after all, God, without her getting all excited. Maybe there's hope. Good night, God!

FUTURE

God, today I met with my guidance counselor. When he looked over my marks, he was surprised I did so well in science and math. He asked me if I had given any thought to what I wanted to do when I graduated. I told him I wanted to be a doctor. He couldn't tell whether I was serious or just joking. "You really want to be a doctor, an M.D.?" he asked me. I said I wanted to be a doctor since I was a little girl. He assured me that if that is what I really wanted, I shouldn't have any problem, because my marks were very good. He said I should start considering the different colleges, so I won't have to shop around at the last minute. He promised to give me all the help I need.

That made me feel good, because even though my marks are good, I was still afraid the guidance people would come up with all kinds of reasons why it would be impossible for me to become a doctor. I'm glad I'm over the first hurdle.

I had Father Angelo in class today. I know he likes me. He even called me by my name. He was called down to the principal's office about some boys who were in a gang war during lunch break. He asked me if I would take charge of the class while he was out. I was thrilled. He has a real tough job. In one class he has fifteen kids who are on parole. One boy hit a teacher last year and knocked him through three rows of desks. He's in Father Angelo's class this year, and some of the "sickoes" are trying to get the kid to see if Father Angelo is afraid of him.

Last week there was this big gang war. Almost two hundred kids were involved. One boy had an artery cut. Almost a dozen ended up with knife wounds. It happened right down the street from the police station, where there's over a hundred cops stationed. Father Angelo told the sergeant there was going to be trouble. The kids told him, hoping he could prevent it in the last minute. But the cops wouldn't go down, so Father Angelo went alone, and he was at least able to break it up before more were hurt. The police finally came, just in time to be interviewed by the reporters.

I think some of the girls were jealous because I was picked to monitor the class for Father Angelo. After class, three of the girls came up to me and asked how come I was picked, and did Father Angelo and I have something going. I wish I could have told them "yes," but, instead, I told them I hardly even knew him.

After school I went looking for a job. My father cut my allowance last week for talking back, so I'm having a hard time getting things I need, especially for the party I'm planning to have in two weeks. Well, I guess I've really rambled tonight, God. You're probably tired of listening to me. I'm tired, too. Good night, God!

WORK

I got a job, God. I'm working in a supermarket, in the produce department. It's fun. I didn't think I'd like working, but I really enjoy it. I don't even know the names of all the vegetables. We eat the same thing week after week at home. I bring different things home each night to experiment with. Some I like, but others, I can see why my mother doesn't cook them. The manager gets a big "kick" out of me trying all the different things. He gives me a real good discount, and says I'm good for business. One of the fruits I really like is fruit from the prickly pear cactus.

Some of the kids from the school come to the store, , and want me to give them extra. I don't know what to do. I don't want to hurt their feelings, and I don't want to lose my job either. Most of the time I just make believe I think they're joking, but if they're from poor families, I give them extra without letting them know about it. I don't think that's wrong, do you, God?

Now that I've been working for almost two weeks, I still don't have much money saved. I get ninety-two dollars and sixty-four cents take home pay. I bought a new pair of designer jeans, and a blouse and sweater. It cost most of my salary. And to think that I had to work all week just for that makes me sick. I guess Mom and Dad aren't so bad after all. My sister and brother and myself really have a lot. But, it's more fun, God, earning my own money. I feel good about being independent. Good night, God!

PARTY

I feel horrible, God. I had a party for my friends. I should feel good about having a party; I put so much into it. And Mom and Dad were really good about it for once, and even let us have the house to ourselves. But, what a mess, God!

I invited only ten kids over, and we were supposed to have only pizza and one case of beer, that was left for us. We were having a great time in the beginning, but about ten o'clock, some guys came over with two more cases of beer. I should have told them they couldn't come in, but how could I, God? Well, it didn't take long before Eddie started making out with Tom's girlfriend. Tom got mad and told Eddie, "Hands off!" Eddie didn't like it. Besides he was pretty well "smashed." He hauled off and gave Tom a bloody mouth. Then, all hell broke loose. Jack, who's Tom's best friend, hit Eddie and everyone started fighting. My mother's best lamp was broken. Jane got smacked in the mouth. She may lose her front tooth. I got a black eye. Arlene got her blouse torn.

The next door neighbors, or maybe somebody passing by, must have heard the noise, because, in no time the police appeared. They wanted to know where my parents were. I told them I didn't know, but I really did. I was hoping that, by some miracle, everything would be covered up and my parents wouldn't find out about it. How stupid that was!... By the time the cops came, some of the girls had run out the back door, so there were only seven or eight of us left. We were all packed into the police van and herded off to the police station. Oh, God, what an experience! You'd think we were criminals. One cop was real nice. He must have teen-agers himself. But the others were real mean. One guy pushed us around, another hit Arlene for calling him a "pig." After he hit her, I called him a "pig," too. When he went to hit me, Mike grabbed him. Two other cops jumped on Mike and dragged him into one of the cells.

About a half hour later, my parents came in. I was so humiliated. I had tried to act so grown-up, by having my own party, and it turned into the most miserable experience of my life. We were all eventually released, and no charges were pressed, except against Mike. He has to appear in court. I told him I'd go with him and testify on his behalf. The police captain bawled the hell out of my mother and father for not properly supervising their children.

I didn't sleep all that night, God. I felt more sorry for my parents who finally thought I was mature enough to be trusted. They were really let down. They didn't even say anything when we came back from the police station. I guess they were just too crushed. I would have felt better if they had screamed at me. At least I would have felt punished. But the silence was devastating, because I tore myself apart in my own mind. I tossed and squirmed all night. Everytime I thought of something new, I tossed again. The night seemed endless. I dreaded facing my parents in the morning. I would rather have stayed in jail than go through the self-torture I suffered that night. I didn't even think to talk to you about it, God. I was beside myself.

But now it's almost a week since it happened, and I'm beginning to be myself again. The next morning at the breakfast table I could tell my mother and father hadn't slept either. My brother and sister were afraid to say a word. I tried timidly to break the ice by apologizing and telling Mom and Dad that they trusted me to be grown-up and I failed them. I tried to be strong, but I couldn't. I broke down and cried. Still they said nothing. It was horrible. I got up from the table and went upstairs. They still said nothing. I couldn't stand the tension. It was too explosive. I got my coat and quietly went down the back stairs and left the house.

I didn't know where to go. It was Sunday morning and the streets were empty, except for a handful of people on their way to church. I just wanted to be by myself. As I walked near the church I decided to stop in, more to distract myself than to go to Mass. I got the surprise of my life when I saw Father Angelo saying the Mass. Did you plan it that way, God? It's things like that that make me think that you're really aware of things. Father Angelo never said Mass in our church before. If he did I surely would have heard of it at school the next day.

I sat in the back seat and cried, partly from exhaustion, partly from guilt, and partly from sheer thrill at the realization that you arranged for Father Angelo to be there, and for me to stop in, which I never do. Then I sat back and just watched him, every movement and every word. Slowly, I began to feel peaceful, almost tranquilized, perhaps, hypnotized.

The sermon seemed like it was meant just for me. You don't know how I felt, God. But I guess you do; you planned the whole thing, though I hope the party wasn't part of it. Well, in the sermon he talked about "how complicated life is for young people today. Everything used to be simple and unsophisticated when people were poorer. Even adults didn't do much partying. Now, everybody parties and everybody drinks. It's the "in" thing to do. Kids try to imitate and fall flat on their faces because they haven't developed the art of being sophisticated. It used to be the rare kid that got picked up by the police, but now it seems the rare kid who isn't picked up. Life is too complicated and too fast for young people. They can't learn that fast and, as a result, make a lot of mistakes, some of them serious, before they learn how to cope.

"But grown-ups have to understand that kids are not evil. They are no worse and no better than the kids of other generations. We as adults can't put the blame on them for trying to act like grown-ups and imitating the sick lifestyle that we have learned to live so gracefully. They need our help and our guidance which we never have the time to give them. And, very often, it's a stranger who has the greatest influence on the kids' life. Many a boy and girl prays secretly in the quiet of their hearts, without anybody knowing it, because they don't feel comfortable worshiping in church with people whose lifestyle they try to imitate but secretly despise."

You don't know, God, the effect those words had on me. It was as if you yourself were talking to me, telling me you understand, and that I really shouldn't tear myself apart with guilt. All during the rest of the Mass I felt so close to Father Angelo. I felt as if you had put him into my life, and that, in some special way, he was mine. I realized then that I loved him. Good night, God. Thanks for everything. I think you're wonderful, even if I can't imagine what you look like.

INJUSTICE

God, somethings I just can't understand. We had this real great teacher for chemistry. Everybody likes him, and we all do well in his class, except maybe for the slower kids. But, even they like him a lot because he helps them, and they do better in his class than in the other classes. Today the principal fired him. Some of the girls heard the principal arguing with him in the office this morning and we had no chemistry teacher this afternoon. We were told he was no longer teaching at our school.

We had a meeting with the student council officers after school and asked them to talk to the principal. When they did, the principal told them it was none of their business. They said it was their business since the students' classes were involved, and all the students liked that teacher. The principal told them to leave his office.

We all know the real reason why they got rid of him, God. He was just too good and showed up the other teachers. A lot of the teachers don't give a damn about the kids. They just put in their time, collect their paychecks, and don't care whether the students pass or flunk. But, this teacher was different. He used to do a lot of extra work with the students who had problems. It embarrassed the other teachers who couldn't get out of the school fast enough in the afternoon. They got the union after the principal, and he came real hard on him and told him he was getting the other teachers upset by being a maverick. He told him to leave earlier after school. When he told the principal he couldn't do it in conscience, the slower kids needed help, the principal lost his cool and told him there was going to be trouble. Arlene got all this from her aunt who works in the principal's office.

When dirty tricks like this happen, it makes me disgusted with school. The kids don't really count. The ones who always get the rotten deal are the average and below average students. Schools are aimed for college, and if you aren't college material you're nothing. They may have some watered down courses for the slower students, just because they have to teach them something, but the kids are bored to death. A lot of those kids have real talent. You should see some of the pictures they draw. Well, maybe you shouldn't; they are not the type you'd like to look at, but they are really good, and they certainly didn't learn it from the corny art classes they have only a couple of hours a week. And some of those kids have their own bands, and they are good, too. And one boy put his own car together from parts he got from a junk yard, and it's beautiful, and it runs, too.

These kids would have a great time in school if they were taught the things they were good at, like the students who are going to college. They get everything. Mike's a boy in my class. He's great at woodcarving. They don't teach it in school. It's too bad. Mike could learn to make furniture and all kinds of fancy things. He'd be already to go into business when he graduates. But, he's not going to be prepared for anything. And those kind of students are the majority.

Parents should demand justice for their kids, but they're probably afraid to buck the system. I guess nobody really gives a damn. You must really get disgusted with this screwed up world. Either that or you're got some sense of humor. Good night, God!

THINGS

There are so many beautiful things in the world, God. I guess you know that, but I'm just beginning to realize all the mystery and fascination in simple things around us. I learned a lot in biology about plants, and find crossing plants fun. I got these six tuberous begonia plants a couple of years ago and have cross-pollinated them in different ways. Now I have the most beautiful combination of colors.

My science teacher said in class last week that eventually science will take all the mystery out of creation as scientists dissect the complicated processes of living things. That seems stupid to me, God. The mystery isn't in finding out how nature works, but in putting it all together. Kids take a lot of things apart, but they aren't too good at putting them back together again. Scientists remind me of grown-up kids who get their kicks out of destroying all the fun and beauty in creation by laying bare the mysteries, but it's laughable when you realize they can't put it all back together again, God. I guess you're pretty good after all, you put it all together from nothing. I'm really tired tonight. My knee hurt all day. I hope it's nothing serious. Good night, God.

LOVE

Mike and I have become very close the past couple of

months, God. We've been seeing each other quite a bit, lately, and I've grown very fond of him. I even think of him when I'm going to sleep at night, and wish he was lying next to me. How beautiful it would be!

We were on a date last Saturday night. We went dancing and then went out with the gang, like we usually do. After we left Gino's, Mike asked me if I wanted to go over to his house for a while. Even though it was late, I really wanted to go, so I talked myself into it. When we got there his mother and father weren't home. Mike said they went to a party and wouldn't be home until late. So, he turned on the stereo and we sat and talked. He asked me if I wanted a drink. His father had all kinds of stuff in the bar. I knew I shouldn't have taken it, God, but I was trying to act grown-up again and thought I'd be sociable.

We talked and sipped our drinks and I began to feel all warm inside. Mike put his arm around me and told me how much he loved me and how much I meant to him. I loved it when he told me those things. I told him I was really fond of him, too, and that I miss him very much when I don't see him. He put his head on my shoulder and kissed my neck. It made me tingle all over. We both fell back on the floor, and he kissed me real hard. His strong body felt so good next to mine, God, and I realized how much I loved him.

It was beautiful, but then he started to do things that got me all confused. I finally realized I had been "conned." What was happening wasn't as spontaneous as I thought. I began to get frightened as he got more insistent. I now knew the whole scene had been calculated, even to the drinks. I resented it. I wasn't the first one either; that was obvious. He had more experience than I had thought.

He sensed I was uncomfortable and tried to smooth-talk me. But it made things worse. I wondered if he even loved me. I was determined I was going to get out of this mess even if I had to fight with him. He became more insistent, and I got angry. I'd be damned if I was going to be just another conquest. The only way I could really keep him would be if I wasn't a pushover. I guess he saw I was getting tense and when I turned my face away, he asked me what was the matter. I told him I thought we should stop, and that I really should be getting home. He got really angry, God, and said something that wasn't too nice. I was surprised and suspected even more that he didn't really love me. I could tell; he didn't feel the same kind of love for me that I had for him. I felt disgusted for letting myself get trapped into this.

I was late getting home that night, God, and that produced another scene. It's tough being a teen-ager. You have to keep everything to yourself, and it's hard not to get angry with parents when you're going through hell inside and they're yelling and screaming at you for something entirely different. I don't blame some kids for not being able to handle it. I just wanted to get away from everybody that night. The thought even crossed my mind to run away. But, I tried to keep my "cool." I had a lot to think about that night, God, and I stayed awake for a long time. I should have talked it over with you then; I probably would have felt much better. I guess that's why I talk to you so much, God, because I really don't have anybody else I can talk to about these things, and I do feel better after I tell you. Good night, God, and thanks for being a friend. I think a lot more about Father Angelo now that I have problems with Mike. Do you think it's all right?

CHURCH

I tried to be nice, God, and went to church this morning, but it was such a bore. I don't understand anything that's going on. I don't know why priests have to wear those "fruity" clothes. Even the prayers seem artificial. Nothing seems to touch my life, and I can't see how it brings people closer to you, God. In fact, I think it makes you seem very far away. I feel closer to you when I talk to you the way I do. It means a lot to me, God, to be able to talk to you, and I know you care.

This afternoon we went to my cousins. They live about an hour's ride from here. It was a beautiful day. The snow had started to fall, just enough to cover the ground and the tree branches. It was nice riding through the snow. Even my father was in a good mood for a change. It seemed everybody was, because for once Bobby and Cynthia didn't ruin everything by starting a big hassle.

It was almost one o'clock when we arrived. As soon as we got out of the car my cousin Lorraine ran out the front door, and across the lawn, and threw her arms around me. We hugged each other. Both of us had tears in our eyes. We hadn't seen each other for a long time. We had been friends since we were kids. We used to share everything: candy, ice cream, toys, our childish problems, heartaches, and our fun. Even after her family moved from our neighborhood, we still remained just as close as ever. I can't describe the happiness I felt when I saw her. It was the first time in over a year.

After everyone said hello and we went inside, Lorraine and I went up to her room and filled each other in on everything that had happened since we last saw each other. I even told her about my knee, God, which has really been hurting lately. She's the only one I told about it, except you. I'm beginning to worry about it because hardly a day goes by that I don't have a lot of pain.

By the time dinner was ready we had talked about school, boyfriends, sports, clothes, music, hair styling, hobbies, the future, you name it. It was great. We had roast pork for dinner, and baked apples, which are my favorites. The rest I forget. I didn't care much for it anyway.

It was late when we got home, and even though I'm tired, I wanted to tell you all about today, because it was a beautiful day and I wanted to share something nice with you for a change.

HATE

God, for the first time in my life I think I really hate somebody. You know my friend Arlene? Well, we got this real miserable teacher; she's a real "sicko," and for some reason she has it in for Arlene. This afternoon Arlene asked to be excused. The teacher said no. Arlene started to explain, but the teacher shut her up and told her to sit down. Arlene's been having a real problem, which was very embarrassing to have to explain in front of the whole class, if you know what I mean.

So, Arlene got up and started to walk towards the door. The teacher was furious and ran over to stop her, just like a juvenile. She tried to stand in the doorway and told Arlene to sit down. Arlene got really mad. She pushed the teacher and she fell on her rear. The whole class laughed like hell. I suppose it wasn't nice to laugh, but we couldn't help it. She deserved it; she's mean. She shouldn't even be teaching.

Well, it didn't end there. The teacher immediately went to the principal's office and told her version of the story. Arlene was called to the office and wasn't even asked for an explanation. The principal dismissed her from school. And Arlene's a good student, too. This will ruin her whole year.

God, I feel such hatred for that teacher because Arlene is my real good friend. I've been trying to think of ways to get even with her and get her fired. I've never felt this way about anybody, God, and I don't like myself for it, but I can't live with that feeling inside me. Maybe you can tell me what to do. Hatred is terrible, and if I can help Arlene without getting revenge, maybe I'll feel better. Good night.

NEXT DAY

When I got up this morning, God, I had this great idea. I decided to go to the principal and explain everything to him about Arlene and me being very good friends, and about Arlene having serious problems every month lately, and how the teacher has been miserable to Arlene all year long and all the kids in the class have been talking about it. I did tell him everything and told him it's not just Arlene.

I think the principal believed me,   because after school the teacher was in the principal's office for the longest time. She was still there when basketball practice ended. I hope they let Arlene come back. She's really a good kid.

I feel a lot better, God, than I did last night. Hatred is a real sick feeling and it doesn't even accomplish anything except tear your insides out. I hope I never feel that way again because I can't handle it. I guess the best way to deal with those bitter feelings is to look for real solutions that will do some good without hurting anybody. I guess you helped me to see it that way, because I certainly didn't think that way last night. Thanks.

I saw Mike today. It was the first time since that Saturday night. He was cool to me; he seemed embarrassed. We talked for a while. I think he wanted to ask me out, but didn't. I feel differently about Mike lately. I still love him, but I don't think he loves me the same way, and I think he's going to drift, so I'm trying to prepare myself for the big letdown.

My leg is beginning to hurt more and more every day. It kills me when I jump for a basket. I think it's really serious, God. I always wonder if it started the day I was nicked by the car. It's hurt ever since and in the exact same place. Help me, God, I'm frightened. Good night. God, what was Jesus like? I wonder a lot about him lately.

TRAGEDY

God, you won't believe this but Arlene was back in school today. The teacher didn't look too happy though. But, then, she's never happy anyway. I didn't tell Arlene anything. That's just between me and you. I guess you do answer prayers.

We had a basketball game this afternoon. Something terrible happened, God. I was jumping to put in a shot and when I came down my leg gave out and I fell. The pain was excruciating and I guess I must have fainted. I don't know how long I was out. When I woke up, Father Angelo was kneeling on the floor next to me. There was a big crowd around me. Father had his hand on my forehead and asked me what happened. I told him I had this pain in my knee for a long time and it's been getting worse. He told me not to move and said the doctor was coming. I was afraid I might have to go to the hospital. And I did, God. That's where I am now.

Father Angelo came in the ambulance with me. He held my hand all the way, and when I looked up at him, he had tears in his eyes. I knew he loved me, and even though I was in terrible pain, I felt happy.

The doctor came in several times. Every time he touched the knee it hurt. When he asked me what happened, I told him. He said he was going to have it x-rayed to see if there was any serious damage. About an hour later, two nurses brought me down to radiology.

After supper the doctor came back. He looked grim. I got scared. I knew something was seriously wrong. When I asked him what was wrong with my leg he said he wasn't sure. Then he took my parents outside, (they had been with me all afternoon), and talked to them privately. Father Angelo had left just a few minutes before, but said he would come back when he finished his work.

After what seemed eternity, my parents came back from talking with the doctor. I asked them what was wrong and they had trouble telling me. Then I realized it was serious. They said the x-rays showed shadows in the bone area of the knee. It seemed to indicate an infection of some type but the doctor wasn't sure. He would have to do a biopsy. But that could wait until tomorrow.

It was seven thirty. My parents stayed a little while longer, then left. Nobody bothered me the next hour. I thought about many things: my basketball playing, my classes, Christmas vacation, what was really wrong with my knee, Father Angelo, Mike, a lot of other things.

While I was daydreaming, Father Angelo came into the room. He walked over to the bed and kissed me on the forehead. He asked me if the doctor had come back. I told him everything I knew, but he showed no reaction. I could tell he was used to hiding his feelings. He went to the other side of the room, brought a chair back to my bedside and sat down. He just looked at me for what seemed a long time, obviously deep in thought.

I asked him who won the game. He said we did. I was glad of that. Then he added that the score wasn't as high as usual because the star player was missing. I was surprised he even noticed. I was curious about a lot of things and asked him what he does when he's not teaching. He told me about his work and the various committees he's on. It sounded fascinating. I had always thought a priest's life must be boring.

He asked me why I didn't tell someone about my knee sooner. I said I thought it would go away; I never paid that much attention to aches and pains. I told him about the incident with the car and how it nicked my knee, and ever since I had problems with it, but nothing I couldn't handle, until today.

Then the nurse came in, God, and said she had a sleeping pill I had to take. While she was taking my temperature she glanced at Father Angelo, and with a big grin on her face, asked, "Your boyfriend?" I jokingly smiled, "Yeah." She took my temperature and left. Father Angelo left a few minutes later. I felt sad. I thought about him for the longest time, and I guess that brings me to where I am now, God. It was a difficult day. I hope you help me because I'm really worried this time. Good night!

HOSPITAL

I didn't sleep much last night, God. Even the sleeping pill didn't help. The doctor came in early this morning. He had two other doctors with him, and even though I had never been a patient before, I could tell this wasn't ordinary for just a simple problem. I sensed it was something serious. They felt my knee and looked for a long time at the x-rays and talked to each other in terms too technical for me to understand. One word they used repeatedly was carcinoma. I asked a nurse later on what it meant and she said it had many meanings, which she was too busy to go into, but she'd talk to me about it when she had a chance.

They sure don't give you much food in the hospital, God, and it tastes so flat. Lunch wasn't too bad, but, then I don't usually eat lunch anyway. I slept for a while after lunch. When I woke up, Mike was sitting right near the side of my bed. He was just looking at me. He told me how beautiful I looked, lying there so peacefully. He kissed me and said he missed me terribly. He told me he had called my house last night to ask my mother how I was, but she said they really didn't know. The doctor was confused as to what was really wrong. They'd have to do tests.

It was good to see Mike. I missed him, too. I really do love him very much. When I think about that night, I know maybe I shouldn't, but I wish I'd have let him continue. I wouldn't have been as miserable as I've been the past few weeks. Our relationship has been different ever since, and Mike's been seeing Janet between classes. She is one of his old girlfriends.

Mike stayed until about four, God. He held my hand most of the time, and we kissed every chance we got, which wasn't very much because the nurses and aides kept coming in and out all afternoon. He said he'd come back after supper.

The doctor came in during the day and took some material from inside my knee. He said he was going to have it analyzed to see what was really wrong, but wouldn't have an answer for a day or two. I asked him if he would let me know no matter what it turned out to be. I told him I wouldn't be upset even if it was serious. He said he'd see, then left.

Mom and Dad came in just after Mike left and again after supper. They brought me a lot of things, so I knew I was going to be here for a while. I could tell by the kind way they treated me that they were both deeply worried about something, though whenever I asked them what the doctor said they would merely tell me he was not specific, and wouldn't know for a few days. I didn't press them. Mom left some homemade cookies. It was a long day, God. Good night.

HOSPITAL - SECOND DAY

I hate just lying in bed, God. The doctor left orders for me not to stand on the leg that hurts. He said the bone seems very fragile according to the x-rays. So, I have to stay in bed most of the time, though the nurse lets me sit in the lounge chair occasionally.

Mike didn't come back last night. I looked out in the hall every time someone passed, hoping it would be Mike. When visiting hours were over, I knew he wouldn't be coming. I don't know why he didn't come. I hope he wasn't out with Janet.

There's this one nurse I have; she's really miserable. Most of the nurses are careful when they move me in bed, to change the linen or something. But, this one is mean. She knows my leg hurts a lot, yet she's rough when she makes me move around. She tells me to hurry up and stop feeling sorry for myself. I don't think I feel sorry for myself, God. I had this pain for months and didn't let anybody know about it. And sometimes it hurt a lot. One of these days I'm going to tell her off.

It's almost Christmas, God, only a few days left. I hope I don't have to spend Christmas in the hospital. This place is so depressing. I'd rather stay in bed at home than spend Christmas here. And the doctor didn't give me any satisfaction when I asked him today. He was in a rotten mood himself and just put me off when I questioned him. He said he'd be back tomorrow.

I was happy when I saw Mike this afternoon, God. I was afraid he might have been losing interest in me, but he seemed to be his old self. I was sitting in the chair when he came in. He sat down next to me and kissed me, and we held hands. I told him I wished we could be alone together. I wanted so much to show him I loved him. His team has been doing great. They haven't lost a game all season. My team lost the last game. Mike said the girls really missed me at the games. I guess that's the reason they haven't been in to see me.

Mike asked if I was going home for Christmas. I told him I didn't know yet. The doctor might let me know in a day or two. Mike's having a big party over at his house the day after Christmas. I hope I can make it. The whole gang's going to be there; it should be a blast.

God, I'm really starting to get depressed about my knee; nobody tells me anything. Whenever the doctor has something to say to my parents, he always takes them out into the corridor. He must think I'm stupid or something. Even my mother won't tell me anything. I know it has to be real serious now. Even my brother and sister are being nice to me. Everybody's being nice, too damn nice. It's disgusting.

Father Angelo came in today. I don't know what it is about him, but all he has to do is walk through that door and look at me, and I get all butterflies inside. I never felt that way about anyone before, not even Mike. He stayed the longest time. He was sitting close to the bed, and while we were laughing over something funny I accidentally put my hand out and rested it on his. He lifted his hand and held mine. I felt such peace. I looked up at him and our eyes met. I know I had love in my eyes. I could see it in his. He smiled briefly and began to talk about school. He asked me if I was keeping up on my school work. I shouldn't let myself get behind, and even if I have to stay in the hospital for a while, I could still keep up with the class.

He told me he prayed for me every morning at Mass. I told him I don't pray or go to church, but I talk to God practically every night, and sometimes I talk to God about him. He blushed. I don't know what possessed me but I told him I loved him. He seemed a little embarrassed and told me I was very special to him, and he was expecting great things of me. I asked him what kind of things; he said he'd tell me someday. I also told him I thought Jesus must have been like him, and that I really wondered a lot about what

Jesus was like. He promised to talk to me about Jesus the next time he came to visit.

When he left, he bent over and kissed my cheek. I turned my head slightly and our lips touched. He kissed me. I felt so empty when he left, but so happy we had finally come close to each other. I thought about him for a long time after he left. Good night, God.

HOSPITAL - THIRD DAY

Today had to be the worst day of my life, God. The doctor came in this morning and told me the results of the biopsy. He said I had a very serious infection, a rather unusual type of disease. The bone around the knee area was badly affected, and as a result, was brittle and fragile. With the slightest twist of my body and any amount of pressure the bone could crack. I was totally devastated, but didn't show it. I could tell he was impressed.

I asked if he was telling me everything, and he said everything he knew so far. I felt a morbid kind of relief; at least I was spared any more anxiety and worry about what it might be. When I asked him if the knee would heal so I could play basketball soon, he said he couldn't tell how long it would take, but he doubted if I could play anymore this year. I asked him if I could go home for Christmas. He said definitely not. He was too much afraid I might crack the bone if I was the slightest bit careless. It was useless to argue.

My mother and father visited as usual. They told me pretty much the same thing the doctor told me, but their stories differed just enough to make me wonder again if they were keeping something from me. Mom brought my books from school. I was glad in a way. It would keep my mind busy. And I was determined I was going to do well this year since this year's results were the ones that would go to the colleges.

Some of my girlfriends came in after school today. They were really great. They were the only ones who didn't get all mushy about my being sick, and we had a good time. The nurse had to come in and tell us to cool it; we were disturbing the other patients. The girls brought all kinds of funny little things they had bought at the novelty store. We had a lot of laughs over them as they decorated the room.

Mike came in while the girls were here. They made a big fuss over him, the way they usually do. Mike's really popular. I'm lucky to have him as a boyfriend. He kissed me as usual, but just joined in with the girls, as we all fooled around. He had a package which I didn't see when he first came in. He opened it, and showed me the prettiest roses I had ever seen. When the nurse came in, I asked her if there was a vase around somewhere. She said there was a whole closet full. In a few seconds, she came back with one. We put the flowers in it, arranged them nicely and put them on the window sill. I gave Mike a big kiss, and told him how beautiful they were.

The girls were discreet and, after a few minutes, kissed me goodbye and left, but not before they made some suggestive remarks to Mike. Mike and I were alone for a while. It was good to see him. He was concerned about my illness, and asked if the doctor gave any indication how long I might be in the hospital. He was also wondering how long I would be laid up. I wanted to tell him good news, but there wasn't any. I could tell he seemed disappointed, but I couldn't tell whether it was because of concern for me. There was an ambiguity about his reaction. I began to feel let down. I couldn't help but feel that there was something strange about Mike's love for me. And yet I love him, God, more each day. I wish we could have fun together, like all the other kids. And I wish our relationship could blossom into something beautiful, but there seems to be something missing.

My family came in this evening, nothing unusual. We had a nice visit. They brought some little gifts. My brother and sister were very much concerned. We've become a lot closer since I got sick. God, I'm terribly tired tonight. Please make me better. Good night.

JESUS

God, I felt really miserable when I woke up this morning. I had this horrible feeling I was never going to get better. Even the sun shining through the window didn't dispel the gloom. That miserable nurse was on duty and I wasn't in the mood for any of her "crap", so when she started in, I let her have it. I told her she must really be an unhappy bitch, because there's not a patient on the floor who can stand her. She said it was because she was so efficient. I told her it was because she was inconsiderate and mean to everybody. If she didn't like helping people, she should quit. She was really upset, God, but she deserved it, and I was glad I said it.

In the early afternoon, Father Angelo came in. Everything seemed to brighten up. He bent over to kiss me. I felt we were friends now, so I boldly turned my face towards him and we kissed. I felt my heart skip a beat; I was so excited.

He sat down by the bed. We talked about a lot of things. I reminded him he promised to tell me about Jesus. He asked me if I really wanted to know. I said yes. When he talked about Jesus, his face radiated joy. He said most people don't really understand Jesus. They create their own Jesus, and it's usually a sick caricature. The real Jesus was very earthy. When everyone else went home at night, Jesus went off into the woods or the hills, and slept under the trees. He loved nature, and felt very close to the animals and the birds. He had absolutely nothing and he was content. He ate what people gave him each day, or he and his friends picked fruit and vegetables from the orchards and fields along the road, and lived on that some days. But Jesus was a very happy person. He couldn't see why people were so obsessed with worry about their future. He said his Father in heaven cared so much for us, that he doesn't let anything happen without a purpose. We should trust him.

I asked him if Jesus was human, or was he God. He said "Jesus always existed as God, but to show his love for us, he came to earth and chose to live just like us. As a man, he had a perfectly balanced personality. He was kind and gentle, yet he was strong and very tough. He could never see anyone hurting without helping them. But when it came to himself, he didn't seem to care. Every morning, when he got up, he knew what he was going to face that day, but he never wavered; he had complete trust that his father knew what he was doing in arranging his life for him. Even when people were miserable to him, he understood their own emptiness and misery, and was kind. He didn't have any petty hang-ups or any phony illusions about himself, so he didn't let people hurt his feelings. He was absolutely beautiful. Strong, hardened men liked him. Little children loved him. They used to jump all over him. Women fell in love with him. Mary Magdalen was a prostitute. When she met Jesus, she was so completely devastated by him, it changed her whole life."

God, we must have talked for almost two hours, but the time passed so fast, it seemed like only a few minutes. Jesus must have really been wonderful, God. Is he still real? Is he still the same as Father Angelo described him? I think I could like him, God. He really seems like my type. You won't be hurt if I talk to him instead of you, will you, God? He seems more real. I have a hard time thinking about you because I can't picture you. But Jesus seems so human.

Maybe that's why you sent him to us, so he could be our friend, and Father Angelo said the two of you are one anyway, so in talking to him I am talking to you, too. I feel very close to you, God. You have been the only one I could tell about all that's happened to me the past few months, and I know you listen to me. But, I find it hard to understand why you let this horrible thing happen to my knee. Please make me better. Good night, God!

FRIENDS

Jesus, this is new to me, talking to you. Father Angelo talked to me about you and I think you're not too bad. I know you and God are the same so I guess I'm still talking to God.

Well, today I got a letter from my cousin Lorraine. She's always been my friend, Jesus. I already told her about my knee when I was down to visit last month. She's got all her Christmas presents ready and can't wait until Christmas. She's more religious than I am, Jesus, and she really looks forward to Christmas. She even celebrates Advent. She has this little paper tableau which she's had since she was a kid. It has little windows in it and you open one each day for the twenty-five days before Christmas. Behind each window is a picture symbolizing a prophecy. The last window covers the picture of the Nativity. She really enjoys that kind of stuff, but her family was always different from ours. We were never big on anything like that in our family. We don't even go to church much less celebrate the seasons.

But, it was fun hearing from her. She's very concerned about my illness, and said she's praying for me every day. She said she just knows I'm going to be all right. Well, Jesus, I hope she's right, because I sure don't feel that way. The way everybody acts around here, I wonder if I'm ever going to walk again. Father Angelo said you're just the same now as you were when you lived on earth. He said you were kind to people who were in bad shape. Well, Jesus, I sure am in bad shape, and I hope you don't forget me, because I'm really down. I suppose I don't have a right to ask you for any favors, you never meant much to me before, and I feel sort of funny asking you for favors right off, but I am so worried that I have a disease that's not curable, and I can't bear the thought I'm going to be a cripple all my life.

I also got some cards from some of my friends today, Jesus. It makes things a little more cheery to see pretty cards hanging on the wall. I don't know what I'd do without my friends; they make me feel like everybody cares, and that I'm not going through this all alone. Even though they can't do anything to help, it still makes me feel good that they care.

Some of my teachers came in today. They've been really nice. I'm surprised how human most of them are. They're sure a lot different than in school. But, I suppose they have to put on an act in school to keep discipline. I appreciate the little presents they brought; nothing very costly, but a lot of thought in them. I feel a little bad I couldn't stand some of them in class; they've been the nicest ones since I've been in the hospital.

I've been keeping up on my school work. I even take the tests and do well in them. The teachers said I shouldn't have any trouble passing at the end of the year. I'm at least glad about that.

Well, Jesus, it's been a long day and I'm tired. My knee hurts terribly. Good night.

DAY BEFORE CHRISTMAS

Jesus, what a confusing day it was. Everybody's in a Christmas mood, and running around happy, except the miserable old prune. I wonder if she even celebrates Christmas. The nurses had a little party in my room today. It was really great of them. I guess it's because I've been here longer than anybody, and they sort of feel like I'm a part of the place. But, it was nice of them; they didn't have to do it. They even chipped in and bought me the prettiest stuffed puppy I ever saw. That was my first Christmas present. I felt bad I didn't have anything to give them.

Mike came in this afternoon. He didn't stay long; it was busy around here, and he didn't feel too comfortable. He also had to do some last minute shopping. He gave me a present, and told me not to open it until tomorrow. I'm dying to know what it is. He didn't know if he'll be able to come tomorrow, so he'll have to wait until the day after Christmas for his present, because Mom isn't bringing my things until tomorrow.

I was hoping all day Father Angelo would come in, but he didn't. I guess it's a busy day for him. I hope he has a happy Christmas; he sure deserves it for all the nice things he does for others.

The doctor came. He was pleasant, and even wished me a Merry Christmas. It was nice of him because he's Jewish. When he left, I found a present lying on the chair near the bed. At first I thought he may have left it by mistake, but it had my name on it. I opened it and found a beautiful wood carving of the Nativity. It's adorable. I wondered why he thought I would like that for a present. I didn't think anyone would consider me religious.

Mom and Dad didn't come in today, but Bobby and Cynthia came just before suppertime. We were never too close before, but lately we've become good friends. I guess brothers and sisters are too busy fighting to realize what good friends they really could be underneath it all. I'm glad we can finally have intelligent conversations. I didn't realize how serious they can be, and how grown-up they've become. I'm really beginning to like them, Jesus. I hope they talk to

God; it can do so much for them. It's done a lot for me, and they won't get it anywhere else. There's not much religion in our family. I wish I could talk to them about it, but I guess it would sound "corny" coming from me.

Jesus, for the first time in my life Christmas means something to me. It never did before. In spite of all the mess, with my leg and everything, I'm excited about Christmas, about it being your birthday. The only thing is, I don't have anything to give as a present. But maybe the fact that I really feel alone and need you is all you want anyway. I hope that makes some sense, because it's all I have to give.

Jesus, I'm terribly tired. And it's after midnight. Happy birthday, and I hope people are nice to you today. Good night!

CHRISTMAS

Jesus, today was beautiful. Even though my leg hurt more than ever. I didn't mind it too much. Early this morning, the nurse on duty came in and said there was a priest outside with Communion, and asked if I wanted him to come in. I told her to let him in. What a shock when I saw Father Angelo walk through the doorway! He wished me a Merry Christmas and apologized for being so early, but wanted to come before it got too busy at the church. He thought I might like to receive Communion. I told him I hadn't been to confession in years, and he said he could take care of that, too, if I wanted. I told him, O.K., and he heard my confession. I was surprised how easy it was. Then he prayed with me for a few minutes. Strange, he didn't pray the way priests usually pray; he prayed the way I talk to you, Jesus. It was nice. Then he gave me Communion. I could feel tears in my eyes. I knew you accepted my gift. I was happy. It's little things like that that make me know you're real and that you really care.

He didn't stay very long, Jesus. He said I should spend a few minutes after Communion just thinking, and he didn't want to distract me. I was glad to see him, even for those few seconds. I felt such peace about everything. I never realized how beautiful it could be being close to God, and even though I was so much alone, I felt so rich and so contented.

Even breakfast tasted good, but it was really lousy. "Prune face" came in with breakfast this morning, of all days. Even that didn't ruin my day. In fact, I got the surprise of my life. When nobody was around, she asked if I'd mind if she sat down for a few minutes. I said it was all right. I even wished her a Merry Christmas. When she smiled, I thought her face would crack. But, then, she took a little present out of her pocket, and gave it to me. I opened it. It was beautiful. It was a charm bracelet. It was real old fashioned, and made of sterling silver. She said her mother had given it to her when she was young, and every year on her birthday, would give her a new charm. She wanted me to have it, because it was the most precious thing she had, and she had no girl to give it to. I thanked her with tears in my eyes, and told her I was sorry for the nasty things I said to her. She said she deserved it, and was sorry herself. She told me a little about her home life and how miserable it makes her feel. Her husband left her last year, and her oldest boy was sent to prison last month. He's not really a bad boy, but he's been hanging around with a rough crowd ever since his father left home, and she hasn't been able to do a thing with him. She hopes he straightens out. Father Angelo has been trying to help him; he even went with him to court the day he was sentenced. It helped a little. The judge gave him a lesser sentence than he was going to, since the priest is willing to work with him. They may let him out before the end of next year. She told me she prays for me every night; she knows I must be in a lot of pain, but for some reason knows I'm going to get better, in spite of the seriousness of my illness.

In the early afternoon, my family came in to spend Christmas with me. They brought all kinds of presents and things to eat. We talked, and laughed, and reminisced about last Christmas, and how things have changed in one year, and hoped that next Christmas would be brighter. When they left, Jesus, I was relieved, because I was so tired I didn't really feel like having a lot of company.

It was quiet and gloomy in the hospital after they left. I looked out the window, and watched the snow, until it completely covered the ground and the tree branches. There's a little hill outside my window which goes up to the edge of the woods. Every now and then, I could see a deer wandering into the field, and then slip away between the trees.

I did a lot of thinking after everyone left. There was little activity in the halls, so there were no interruptions until bedtime. I thought about Mike and what kind of a future our relationship would have. I had hoped he would come to visit at least for a few minutes today, but he didn't. I wondered where he spent the day. He graduates this year and will be going away to college. He said he didn't want to go too far, so we would be able to see each other frequently, but I'm afraid that he might drift once he meets new friends.

I thought about the nurse whom I have trouble with. It's a little easier to take her when you realize all the problems she has. Her son's in school with me. He's not too bright, and is one of those kids who would really benefit if he was being trained in school for a job. He's not a bad kid, like his mother said, but the school does nothing for him, and he's bored stiff.

I thought of Father Angelo. I feel so peaceful and serene when he's near me. I wish I could see him more than I do. I used to think he was "fruity"; he's got nice features and he's graceful. But, when when I hear some of the things he does, he must be real tough beneath the peaceful exterior.

I thought about the S.A.Ts. Everybody's supposed to take them to get into college, but I think they're a big money-making business, and I don't think I should have to take them to qualify for college. I really don't think I'm going to take them, because I don't believe in them. Even if they say I have to take them, I still won't. When I apply to the colleges, I'll explain that I don't believe in them, and that my school record should be proof enough of my ability. If they don't like it, tough.

I picked up one of my books from school and came across the word "carcinoma." What a horrible sick feeling I got in the pit of my stomach, when I realized that was the word the doctors were using when they were talking about my knee. Oh, Jesus, I hope I don't have cancer; I don't know if I could handle it. Just the thought of losing my leg, or even worse, of dying. Oh, my God, help me. Please don't let it be cancer. I hope the doctor squares with me tomorrow when I ask him. I have to know. I couldn't take the uncertainty.

Jesus, please stay close to me and help me. I really need you now. I'm so afraid I'm going to panic. I hope Christmas was a good one, Jesus, and people were more thoughtful than usual. The nurse gave me my pill before, and it's beginning to take effect. I do love you, Jesus, and I'll try to be strong; but you have to help me. I know I can't do it alone. Good night!

HEAVY CLOUDS

Jesus, I couldn't wait until the doctor came this morning. As soon as he walked in, I thanked him profusely for the beautiful gift he left me. He looked a little embarrassed. He said he saw it in a store and thought it was beautiful.

Then, I asked him pointblank, if I had cancer. I guess I caught him off guard, because he really didn't know what to say. He sat down and asked me why I asked. I told him, and also said I wasn't a child anymore, and I had a right to know. I could tell by his hesitancy that he was trying to figure a way of answering, which meant that he didn't want to tell me. I pressed further and asked why he was hesitant. He said he was trying to be honest. When he saw there was no way I was going to let up, he began to explain.

The doctors had a big discussion among themselves about just what I did have; they also discussed it with my parents and asked them if I should be told the precise nature of my sickness. Everyone agreed that I shouldn't be told until I began to ask questions myself. Then he told me. Yes, I did have cancer. What was going to happen? He said the cancer was in the bone and had already destroyed a considerable amount of tissue. The remaining bone is very fragile and could easily crack if I put any pressure on it.

I asked him what he intended to do. He said the treatments they were giving me were experimental, and have had some success in some cases, but he couldn't predict. They were hoping the radiation would burn out the diseased tissue, but again don't really know for sure what it will do. They have no way of knowing at this time whether the cancer has spread.

If the treatment doesn't work, then what? At first, he hesitated. Then, when I said it was obvious my leg would have to come off, he merely nodded "yes." He tried to console me. I just listened, Jesus, only half hearing. My thoughts were on a thousand other things. When he saw the tears in my eyes, he told me I was a very courageous girl, and, that we shouldn't rule out God. He said he prayed for me every day, and told me I should pray hard. Maybe God will help. Then he left.

It seemed my whole world fell apart, Jesus. The thought of losing my leg devastated me. I could never run and play basketball again. I'd have to have an artificial leg. I wondered what Mike would do. I decided he should know. He had a right to . I knew Father Angelo knew, so I wouldn't have to tell him.

What if the cancer has already spread. How much time will I have left before I die? Die! I couldn't believe it. Jesus, I still can't believe that I might die. It seems so unreal, like I just woke up from a nightmare. It just can't be.

When my mother and father came in, I broke down and cried. We all cried. I told them I didn't want to die, and I dreaded being a cripple. What horrible options! I got angry with them for not telling me sooner, and letting me think I was going to get better, and for treating me like a child. When they left, Jesus, I was still angry. I was angry at everybody; at the son-of-a-bitch who hit me with the car. If he hadn't been showing off, it would never have happened. I was mad at Mike, at Father Angelo, at the doctors, the nurses, at anybody that had anything to do with me. I was even mad at God, and I still am. I really trusted him, and you too, Jesus, and you've made a damn fool out of me. I tried to do what was right; I even made the mistake of thinking you were my friend, but I should have realized it's all a big "con" game about you being real, and about all this religion "crap." I should have known. Now I feel like a real fool, talking to someone who doesn't even exist, like some little kid playing house.

And I hope you don't exist, because if you do, then you're worse than I thought. You're just a cruel, sick, feelingless "creep" who doesn't even know what it is to have human feelings, much less anything like loyalty. And I thought we had become such good friends, and all along I was just imagining everything. I feel so betrayed, so empty, so abandoned. I hate God, I hate life, I hate everything. Maybe I should die and end this whole wretched mess.

I spent the whole afternoon, Jesus, thinking like this. When Father Angelo came in I just ignored him. He's odd. He just sat down as if nothing happened. He said he was talking to the doctor, and admitted he had known all along. I continued reading my book, making believe I didn't hear a word he said, but he just kept talking, as if he knew I was listening.

"I suppose you're mad at God, too. We like to blame things on God. He doesn't defend himself. It's an easy "cop-out." But, remember, Gloria, God's a lot deeper than we think, and a hell of a lot more concerned about us than we think. Just because he doesn't answer, it doesn't mean he's not listening. So, before you judge God, find out what he's up to, first. At least give him half a chance. He doesn't act stupidly; there's always a well-thought-out plan in the back of God's mind, which he shares with us, eventually, if we're patient enough to give him time to work with us. When God's preparing our lives for something great in the future, the preparation is usually very painful, because we're so ill-prepared for the work God wants us to do. So, before you dump him, give him a chance. In the end, he'll turn out to be your best friend."

As he talked, all I could think was that it was all part of the "con"' game, and he happened to be a better salesman than the rest, which made him more "phony" than all the rest. I wish he'd leave me alone.

When he got up to go, I felt worse. He bent over to kiss me and I turned my head away. He kissed my ear instead and whispered, "I love you," then left. I felt terrible, and more alone than ever. I wondered when he would come back. If he went away for the Christmas vacation, then I wouldn't see him for a week. I couldn't bear it. I wanted to tell the nurse to ask him to come back, but my pride wouldn't let me. I cried. The best friend I have and I had to treat him that way.

Jesus, I don't know why I'm talking to you tonight. I really think we should end it. I don't mean anything to you, and you've never really meant that much to me before; it all seems to be just a fantasy. You don't even seem close anymore. I don't care what happens anyway. Goodbye.

AFTER THE LONG SILENCE

It's been a long time, Jesus, almost two weeks, since I talked to you last. I don't know how to start. I don't know what to say. I missed you. When I went to sleep each night, in the darkness, I could sense your nearness. It was as if you wanted almost to talk to me, but I chose to ignore you. I feel ashamed, and even more ashamed at my motives for talking to you tonight. I don't know whether it's because I have no one else to talk to about things I can't share with anyone else, or whether I really care about you. Maybe a bit of each. But, I have to talk to you. You are all I have now. So many things happened the past two weeks, that I have to get it all straightened out. I can do that better when I talk it over with you. The bad things don't seem so bad, and the good things have more meaning.

Mike came in the day after Christmas. I told him everything. He was shocked. He was sympathetic and concerned. He asked me at least two or three times, while he was visiting, if there was any chance I could get better. It seemed like a strange question. It was as if he wanted to make sure of something. I couldn't understand what he was driving at. He kissed me tenderly before he left, but his kiss had none of the feeling of previous times. I was disappointed.

Arlene came in to visit, you know, the one who got in trouble with the teacher. We're good friends. She brought me a Christmas present, a funny stuffed thing made out of stocking material. It was a funny face. It was clever. We had a nice visit; she brought me up to date on the latest. She said she'd be in again soon.

Father Angelo came in the day after Christmas. I didn't know what to do. He walked over and kissed me as if nothing happened and then sat down. I was ashamed of the way I treated him the day before, but I had a hard time telling him. I just looked at him and put my hand towards his. He held it and looked into my eyes. I just said I was sorry; he said he understood. When he asked me how I felt, I broke down and cried. He came towards me and I threw my arms around him and put my head on his shoulder. He held me close. I told him just how I felt about everything, even how much I loved him. I don't know whether he was shocked; I don't even know why I poured out my heart like that. I've never done it before.

After a while, he sat back, and just held my hand. I could tell he was having a difficult time with his feelings, and didn't want to show me what he was really feeling. I told him that I resented God, and that I felt that God was unfeeling, and didn't really care. He asked me why I felt that way. I told him about my talks with you each night, which he said was beautiful. I replied that God let me down, and seemed not really to care. I felt my friendship with him was a waste.

He tried to tell me that I shouldn't judge God so fast. There were many things in his own life that ripped him apart, and made it seem as if God didn't care, and he got angry with God. He even called God something horrible one time, when he was very upset. The more real God is to you, the more you react to him when things happen in your life, and the freer you are in the way you treat him. I told him it was all ended with Jesus and me. He just laughed and said, "You don't know God; you're not getting away that easy. He haunts you when he wants you, and I think you're very special to him, Gloria. So, don't despair. Be mad at him if

you have to and tell him off, if it helps, but you'll be back
with him before long. Mark my words, he's got a big
investment in you. Your relationship with God is just
beginning."

He went on to tell me that, when he got really angry with
God because things went bad, eventually things worked out
and he was better for it. In fact, as he gets older, he could
see a plan in the way God used him, and then said, that's
really what God does, he uses us, not for selfish reasons, but
to accomplish good things with our lives. After a while you
feel like a fool getting angry with God. He just ignores you
anyway, and goes on with his plans. As he grew older, he
said, he just gave up fighting him. Once he did, his whole
life went smoothly.

He stayed for over an hour talking to me, and even
though I felt good about all the things he said to me, I still
didn't really believe it. And I was determined that it was all
ended between you and me.

But each night, Jesus, it got harder. I could almost feel
you in my room, and I had to fight not talking to you. I even
began to miss my closeness to you. Now I feel ashamed.
You really are the only one I can share everything with.
What happened the next few days made me realize how
much I did need you, and how hard it was to run away from
you. Father Angelo was right. You don't give up.

A few days later, one of my girlfriends told me Mike was
going out with Janet again. I was crushed. I wished she
hadn't told me. I sort of suspected he would, but I didn't
want to know about it. It was a horrible blow, I guess more to
my ego than to anything else. But, it still hurt deeply. I
couldn't help but think that even this was your doing, Jesus,
just to force me to be all alone, so I'd have to come back to
you. I remembered Father Angelo laughing at me, when I
said it was ended between you and me. He must be used to
the way you operate. I still resisted, and was more

determined than ever that you were not going to get the best of me.

Whenever Father Angelo came in, I asked him please not to talk about you. He just smiled, as if he knew everything I was going through. As he held my hand, we talked about many things; about his family, his mother and father, about why he became a priest. We talked a lot about the kids in school, particularly the troubled ones he was always working with. He said he was worried about the dance coming up for the weekend. He heard the kids from across the highway were upset because they weren't allowed in our dances. He was afraid there might be trouble.

I felt proud that he shared his problems with me. It brought us really close. I could have talked to you about it, Jesus, and you might have helped, but I didn't, and I feel responsible for what did happen at the dance. The girls told me about it the next day.

The dance was held as scheduled. There were over two hundred kids from our school at the dance. Everything was peaceful, until there was a big crash at the main entrance, and a whole mob came rushing into the hall. They ran up into the balcony, and started throwing chairs down on top of the kids on the dance floor. Someone called Father Angelo at his house. He came running over and saw some of the gang outside. He grabbed one of them and slammed him against the school building, and asked who was their leader. The kid was scared stiff and told him who it was; the big kid with the leather jacket standing near the entrance. Father Angelo went up to the fellow and, before he knew what hit him, grabbed him by the coat and threw him against the wall. When the kid tried to reach for something, Father put his hands around his throat, and smashed his head against the brick wall. I guess he wasn't too nice about it. He called the boy a son-of-a-bitch and told him to order his gang out of the hall or he'd crack his skull against the wall. The kid was terrified, and did just what he was told. He yelled to the other two boys near the door, to blow the whistle and get them out. "This priest is "nuts" enough to waste me against this damn wall." In no time the hall was emptied. The gang stood around their leader, and asked him what they should do. "Just get the hell away from here, before this guy kills me."

They all started to leave. As they were walking down the street, the police cars converged on the street. Father Angelo told the kid to beat it before the cops came over, and told him he wanted to see him the next day at the rectory. I guess nobody was really hurt, but I feel, Jesus, that I let Father Angelo down. He had shared his worry with me. He was obviously concerned enough to tell me. The only thing I really could have done was to pray, and I didn't even do that. I really feel like a heel when I think about it. He didn't talk about it when he came in the next day. Even when I asked him about it, he didn't say much. I told him I was sorry, and I was afraid for him. He should be careful. He said he wasn't worried. The boys all know he cares for them, and protects them from the police, so they usually cooperate with him, and even come to him with their problems.

I'm all talked out, Jesus, and my knee is really hurting almost more than I can bear. I hope I can get to sleep. Good night!

CHOSEN

I talked to you only briefly the past few nights, Jesus. I was in such pain all day long, I couldn't wait to get to sleep. The last week or so some of the kids have been coming in with their problems. Terri's all mixed-up. She's not the prettiest girl in the world, and she doesn't have any boyfriend. She was complaining today she can't stand boys; they're so egotistical and over-bearing, as if the girls are just waiting for them to notice them. She's really developing a case about boys demeaning women, and using them, and all that. I don't know why she decided to pour her heart out to me. We've never been very close; in fact, I was surprised to see her. I tried to help her, and said she should try not to let boys see she feels this way about them. She's young and has a lot of good qualities, and some day she'll meet a boy who really appreciates her. Then, all the anger and frustration will disappear. I hope I told her the right thing, Jesus. It just seemed like common sense.

Patty came in, too. She's a girl in my class. She's really popular. Lately, her marks have been dropping. She's been getting into trouble at home, and she's beside herself. I asked her what happened to her marks. She said she didn't know. I told her everything was always easy for her before. What changed? She couldn't tell. I sensed something was bothering her that she couldn't talk about. I tried to pry delicately but didn't have much luck. She finally broke down and said she thought she was pregnant. She missed her period and was terrified. She hadn't been taking anything so she was really worried. She asked me what she should do. She was scared stiff to tell her parents. She was afraid to tell her boyfriend. He'd just panic and tell her to have an abortion. She couldn't handle that added hassle. She'd rather try to work the whole thing out by herself without panicking. She asked me how I felt about abortion. I told her I had mixed feelings about it but I thought abortion was gross, and I could never visualize myself having an abortion, no matter what the circumstances. The hell with what people thought; it'd be my life and I'd have to live with it. If I felt I couldn't take care of the baby, I'd give it up for adoption, or maybe I'd work something out with my family. But then, I don't know what I'd feel if something ever happened. Panic changes feelings about everything. The embarrassment, the gossip, the reputation. That's more difficult to handle than the baby.

She said she was glad about what I said because it was the way she felt, too. She said she'd be back again to visit me, and would keep me up to date. I admire her for being so calm about it. She's really trying to do the right thing. I wonder if I'd be that calm. Jesus, I wish you'd help her. She needs you.

Mike came in today, but everything's changed. He seemed sheepish when he kissed me but I didn't say anything. I guess I sort of understand his predicament. But, I still feel horrible about him going out with Janet again. I didn't let on I knew.

Father Angelo has been coming in after school, or sometimes, at night after he finishes work. I've grown so fond of him, Jesus. I don't know how I'd cope with all I've been going through if I didn't have him. I never realized what a good friend a priest could be. I had a long talk to him about suffering and pain, which seems so meaningless. All he said is, "Gloria, you don't know how beautiful you've become since you've been ill. It has refined your whole personality. You see things much more deeply. You've become so understanding of others' problems. Maybe we need suffering to help us develop. God's only concern is that each of us grows as a person. And if God is going to fashion us into something divine, that process can't but be painful. So, don't be discouraged, and, more important, don't give up." I love talking to him. He makes me feel so good inside, as if it's not all a big accident, but that I'm very special to you. I've decided, Jesus, that I'm not going to take any more pain pills. I'm tough enough to put up with the pain. If you decided to save us through your sufferings, then I want to help. You are my friend. Good night!

DOCTORS

Doctors have been coming in more frequently, Jesus. I

guess they're on the verge of making a decision. I told the doctor I didn't want him to prescribe any more pain pills. He was annoyed at first and said I wouldn't be able to stand the pain. He said this kind of pain is very difficult to bear. In fact, he had been prescribing morphine to kill the pain, because he thought that would be the most effective. I felt I really couldn't explain why I didn't want the pills. I didn't think he'd understand. In the end he went along with me. He told the nurse to leave the pills on the table each night in case I changed my mind. So far, I haven't had to take them. Some nights I wasn't able to sleep, Jesus, because the pain was so bad, but I'd get a little sleep during the day. I still think a lot about suffering and what it means, but it's all pretty much a mystery to me.

I realize your view of what's important is totally different from ours. For you what's spiritual is real; for us it's almost make-believe. You may be able to see suffering as necessary to bring good out of us; we see it only as an evil. I suppose, Jesus, if you and I hadn't become so close, I wouldn't have seen any sense in lying in bed all night in agony. I still can't really understand why it was important for you to suffer. But, the fact that it was important to you is enough for me and, since we're friends, I can take it.

The doctor came in yesterday afternoon, Jesus, and said he had just come back from Buffalo. He was talking with the doctors there and they have some new drugs which they feel are worthwhile trying. The side effects, though, are very unpleasant. He asked me if I wanted to take the chance with them. I told him to go ahead. He shook his head and said, "You're a tough one; I've never seen anyone like you in my life. Maybe that's why I like you so much. I wish all my patients were like you. I would be surprised, with your attitude, if we didn't beat this thing."

My mother and father have been coming in every day. So have Bobby and Cynthia. They've been really great. I guess when you come down to it, your family are your best friends, even though, when things are normal, you wouldn't know it. Only one thing, Mom keeps pestering me about taking the pain pills. She just doesn't understand, and even if I explained, she still wouldn't understand. But, I don't get angry with her like I used to. I'm tired, Jesus. Good night!

LIGHT

It's been a lot more cheerful around here lately, Jesus. I guess it's because spring is here and the sun is shining more. I saw the prettiest bird on the windowsill this morning. It was red and brown and yellow. He just stood there for the longest time looking in the window. Then, he flew away.

I'm glad spring is here. I liked the snow for a while, then I got sick of looking at it. It's been so pretty out lately. The leaves have started to come out, and the air seems so clean and fresh again. The nurse opened the window for a while today to let the fresh air in. It was so invigorating. Even the doctor seemed more cheerful.

Father Angelo came in this afternoon. When he kissed me, I held him tight and told him how much I missed him. For the first time he said he missed me, too. Then we talked for about an hour, before he had to leave. I told him to come back soon. When he left, I felt sad.

My friends from school have been coming in practically everyday. Patty was in, you know, the one who thought she was pregnant. Well, it turned out she wasn't after all. But, she and I have become good friends. She's changed a lot lately and is doing better in school. She also decided not to take the S.A.Ts. The teachers were a little upset with both of us, and tried to talk us out of our decision. But, when they realized we weren't going to change our minds, they went along with us. They said our records were good enough, anyway, to be impressive.

The drugs the doctor has been giving me for the past month have been making me very sick. A lot of my hair was falling out, but seems to have stopped. I've been really miserable with all the pain and the nausea and lying in this damn bed all day long. I hope it's worth it. Sometimes, I get so discouraged. I wish it would all end, one way or the other. Good night, Jesus!

GOOD FRIDAY

The spring vacation started today, Jesus. How I wish I could be outside in the fresh air. Even the smell of this place is getting to me. One minute, it's putrid; another minute, it's all antiseptic. I wish I could just stick my head out the window, and take a deep breath of clean air.

It's almost Easter, two more days. Last night, Father Angelo brought me Communion. It was Holy Thursday, the anniversary of the Last Supper, he said. He didn't stay long; he wanted me to spend the time in thought after I received Communion. Today is Good Friday, the day you died, Jesus. I feel as if this whole year was a Good Friday for me. I hope everything I've been going through was a help to somebody, Jesus; otherwise, what a waste!

The doctor was in this morning. For the first time, he said he saw signs of progress. He didn't want to be overly optimistic, and was going to take some more tests next week to verify his observations. Jesus, I hope it's true; I hope I'm getting better. I know it doesn't really seem possible, and the doctor isn't too hopeful, but just maybe, the drugs are working. I realize if you want me to get better, I'll get better. This is the first time I've ever asked, Jesus. Please make me better. There are so many things I want to do with my life. I want so much to be a doctor and to help others. That's what you were, really, Jesus, and I could let you continue your work through me. Now that I've found you, there's so much I want to give to others. I can't wait until the tests next week. I hope they're all negative. Good night, Jesus!

EASTER

Today was Easter, Jesus. I'm glad it was a beautiful day, because I was in a great mood since I woke up this morning. I even slept well last night. The chaplain brought me Communion early, before breakfast, and I felt close to you all day. I really feel like today is the beginning of a whole new life, not just spiritually, but in other ways. I know it's just a feeling but it buoyed me up all day. The pain didn't even seem to hurt as much.

Ever since Christmas, I've been trying to make up to everybody for being so nice to me, so today I had a present for everybody. It wasn't much. For the past month or so, I've been painting these little pictures in oil on 6"x6" canvasboard. They're just simple little things, but each one is different and special for each person. No one realized I was doing it, not even the nurses. A lot of them I did at night, when I couldn't sleep. The nurses gave up making me turn the light off. I really enjoyed doing them, and I was thrilled with the look on everybody's face when I gave them their present.

My family came in and spent most of the afternoon. Also my cousin Lorraine and her family. Even though Lorraine and I wrote a lot to each other since I've been in the hospital, this was the first time the family has been able to come up to visit. We had a long talk, and she said I was more beautiful than ever. I felt bad I didn't have a present for her; I didn't expect her to come.

Father Angelo came in while my family was there. He stayed for a while. I think my family like him. They remarked afterwards about how I beamed when he came into the room. I guess they were a little shocked when I kissed him the way I did. My mother told me after that I shouldn't act that way towards him. She didn't want me falling in love with a priest, and he wasn't that much older than I.

The day went by fast, and I was glad when night came. I was tired. But, I feel really good about today, Jesus. Thanks. Good night!

HOPE

The doctor gave me the tests, and more x-rays early this week. He came with the results today, Jesus. He came in, very seriously, sat down, and began to talk very slowly, and deliberately, as he looked over the papers he had in his folder. My heart pounded with excitement. Finally, he looked up and said, "Gloria, I really can't believe it myself, but there doesn't seem to be any trace of diseased tissue, and new bone tissue is replacing the section that was eaten away. I don't know how long this is going to last, but if it continues, we have a slim chance, one in a thousand, that we'll "lick" this. So, keep up your praying, and hope these drugs work.

Jesus, you can't imagine how I felt. Just to think there's a possibility that I'll recover. I'm so happy. Thanks so much!

LOVE HURTS

Father Angelo and I had a long talk this afternoon. I

finally told him that I think I'm in love with him, and for the first time, he broke down and talked to me about his feelings. He said his superior called him in, and had a long talk with him, and bawled him out for visiting me so often. At the end of the talk, he told his superior that he loved me, and that I was a very extraordinary girl. That made it worse. He told Father he was just immature, and if he wasn't careful, he would jeopardize his vocation.

I asked him if he really loved me. He said he did. But, he said we have to be sensible about this whole thing. I was only seventeen and he was twenty-five. That's a big difference, and we've grown close under unusual circumstances. I told him I loved him even before I got sick. I loved him since the first day he walked into my classroom. He said he felt the same way about me, but it still didn't mean that we couldn't be sensible. I asked him what he meant about being sensible, and he said we should keep our feelings about each other to ourselves, and try to continue the work we're supposed to be doing. I told him that wouldn't make me stop loving him, and he said he knows his feelings will never change towards me, but just let's be careful, so we don't hurt each other. There's so much each of us wants to do with our lives.

I asked him if anything's changed between us, and he said no. I asked him if he was still coming in to visit me as often, and he said yes. Jesus, I want him so much. I hope I'm not being selfish, but I don't want to ever let him go, even if I have to wait until I finish medical school. No one could ever take his place in my life, and I feel you've brought us close to each other for a reason. Jesus, I hope it's not wrong.

I told him the doctor was in and said he noticed improvement. I told him just what the doctor told me. He was thrilled, and said we should keep praying. He looked at me so tenderly. I asked him to kiss me. He did.

When he left a short time later, I felt so empty. I wanted him to stay with me. I thought of him all the rest of the day, Jesus. In fact, I think of him most of the time lately. I even dreamed about him the other night. It was beautiful.

Jesus, I hope I'm not just a crazy, mixed-up teenager, but I'm really in love with him. Don't let me lose him. Good night, Jesus!

MORE GOOD NEWS

The doctor came in again today, Jesus, and said there were signs of more improvement. It's been almost a month since the last tests, and there's been no sign of the disease. The bone is growing back nicely. He said if it continues this way for another month, it should be completely healed. I asked him when I could go home. I couldn't stand it in this place much longer. He said, not until he was sure; at least, not for another month. But, he warned me I shouldn't be overly optimistic. This is very unusual, and he wouldn't be surprised if I had a serious setback.

I'm so happy, Jesus. I know I'm going to get better. I can't wait to go home. I can't wait to sleep in my own bed. I wonder what my room looks like. I'll do it all over. I hope I can play basketball this summer. Oh, I can't wait until I get out of here!

Mom and Dad told me today they had Father Angelo over for dinner. They said he was a lot of fun, and told a lot of jokes. They said he should have been a Jesuit. He's as sharp as a razor. They said they could tell he really likes me a lot, and were glad, but that we had better behave ourselves. I said I loved him too much to hurt him.

I could see a big difference in my family since the doctor gave us the good news. It was as if a heavy load was lifted from everyone's shoulders. There was a cheer, and a lightness to all our conversations again, which had been missing for months. We laughed, we joked, we talked about all kinds of nice things, and even started making plans for the summer, which is just around the corner.

The results of the final exams at school came back. I passed everything; even did better than last year. I was relieved. A whole new world seemed to be opening up. I can't wait to get out of the hospital. The only dark cloud that seemed to be left, was the remark the doctor made about not being surprised if there was a setback. But that was only because he was so surprised at the progress.

I've been so happy lately, Jesus. I have only you to thank for everything, and I am so grateful. I hope I never disappoint you. Good night!

SCHOOL'S END

Jesus, school ended today. I'm now a senior at last. Half my class came in to see me, and we had a real blast. They couldn't stay long, because we were too noisy, but we did have enough time for a party. They all went wild, when I told them what the doctor had said, about my leg getting better, and about my going home in a couple of weeks. They asked if I'd be able to play basketball again; I told them I couldn't even stand up yet, my legs were so skinny. I'd have to have a lot of therapy first, but maybe, by the fall, I'd be back in shape.

The nurses have been wonderful since they heard the good news; you'd think I was their own sister, they seem so happy. They take turns bringing me down to therapy, so I can learn to walk again. I never realized how I took walking for granted. Taking my first steps made me feel like a little baby learning to walk. It seems so simple, but it's so complicated getting everything to work together again. It's almost like a new adventure, but I'm thrilled, just to be able to get out of bed.

A beautician came in today and did my hair. It's all grown back in, and I feel so great with a new hairdo. The lady said she enjoyed working with my hair; it's so soft and easy to style. She asked me what kind of a style I wanted; I told her I didn't really care. I let her play with it and do what she thought I'd look best with. I was glad just to have it look nice again. She said she was going to make me look like a movie star. I told her, "Good luck!"

By the time she finished, it did look nice. I was proud of it myself. I never realized I could look so grown up. The nurses told me I was beautiful, and that I should audition for Hollywood. It made me feel good anyway. It's amazing, what a hairdo can do for one's spirits. It makes you feel almost like a new person.

Father Angelo came in. I was hoping he would, before my hair lost its setting. He seemed sort of absent-minded and asked me where Gloria was. I don't know whether he was serious or just joking. When I laughed, he realized it was me. He told me I was ravishing. He said I looked ten years older, which was just what I was hoping he'd think. I could tell, he liked the way I looked, by the way he kept looking at me.

I was sitting in the chair when he came in. He sat next to me. We just automatically held hands, the way he had for the last six months, but since that was the only form of contact we had, it was amazing how inventive the fingers can be in expressing so much feeling. While he was talking, I kept noticing how subtly and delicately his fingers moved, subconsciously, across my hand, and between my fingers, in hundreds of different patterns, speaking a language all their own, while he was talking to me about something entirely different with his voice. I was listening more to his fingers. They told me such beautiful things, the things I really wanted to hear. He loved me very deeply and tenderly. He was strong, but unbelievably gentle. I could tell that, even though it was against his better judgment, he was not going to let me go, and that even if I had to wait for him for years, we would one day be together. I hoped I was right. I was willing to wait.

He caught me short and said, "Gloria, you're not even listening to me." I said I was, and looked down at his fingers. He blushed. He realized what I meant, and squeezed my hand tight.

He didn't stay too long. I asked him to help me stand up for a few minutes, so I could get some exercise. We walked to the window, and looked out across the field. I told him it would be nice if we could take a walk up there through the woods some day, to see if we could find the deer I used to see during the winter. He didn't answer. He really had to go, but would be back tomorrow. He kissed me. I held him tight and felt him close to me. It was so good. He was strong and masculine underneath the easygoing exterior.

When he left, I felt happy and sad. I was always lonely when he left me, but I knew our love for each other was so deep, that nothing would keep us apart for very long. I was content. I am so happy, Jesus, you brought him into my life. Good night!

FREEDOM

Jesus, I can't wait. The doctor was in today. He had two other doctors with him. They were experts. They all agreed I had no trace of cancer, and were certain I was completely cured. While my case wasn't unique, it was rare that circumstances were so favorable, with the drugs, and getting the sickness in check before it had spread. I was a very, very lucky girl. Even the doctor gave me a big hug and kiss. I thanked him profusely for everything, and told him he would always be my friend. He told me I would be able to leave the hospital in a day or two. Free at last. Oh, Jesus, how my heart leapt with joy! I had finally won the long depressing battle. I realize, Jesus, if it wasn't for you, nothing the doctor did would have worked, and no matter how hard I struggled, it would have amounted to nothing. I have you to be grateful to for everything. I hope I never disappoint you. And I will never again doubt you. I love you so much. Good night!

HOME

Pat came in early this morning, Jesus, to fill me in on everything. One bit of information was rather curious; she had bumped into Mike. They got talking about my coming home. Mike told her that was great. He was talking about having a big party for me. I thought that interesting. But I'm afraid it's a little too late for Mike. I don't feel a thing for him any more. I'll try to be kind to him, but I can't help feeling hurt about our relationship. He really was an eel, Jesus, and I don't want to see him again.

This morning, June 28th, 9:50, I was discharged from the hospital. The sun was shining, when the whole team of nurses and doctors wheeled me down to the front door of the hospital. It was like a big parade, with only the band missing.

My Mom and Dad were waiting there with the car. When I stood up to get into the car, everyone gave me a big hug and kiss, even the doctor. I told them I'd never forget them; they were my family day and night, and I wouldn't have made it without their care and devotion. I love them all.

As the car drove off, I felt a pang of nostalgia, not that I would miss the place, but so many nice people who had done so much for me, and whom I had grown to love, I would probably never see again. But, I guess that's life. I hope you take good care of them, for the way they took good care of me.

When I got home, nothing looked the same. The living room had been done over. My room had all new furniture in it, with a brand new stereo and color TV. There was a beautiful plush rug on the floor and, on the wall across from my bed, a striking picture of the face of Christ. It was gorgeous. I asked my mother where she got it. She told me to look at it close up. It had Father Angelo's name on it. He never told me he painted. I was delighted.

I thought, when I got home, I could get all dressed up, and go out, and walk around the neighborhood. But, I was so tired, I had to go to bed. Imagine, after all that time in the hospital, I spent half of my first day home in bed. I must have slept for hours, because, when I woke up, it was time for supper. Mom's cooking never tasted so good. We had roast pork, my favorite. She even invited Father Angelo over for supper, and sat him right next to me. It looked like he had become part of the family. We had a great time.

The evening went fast, Jesus. After we had talked over all the events of the past six months, it was close to midnight. Father Angelo left about 11:30. After that, we all got ready for bed. It was a perfect day. Thanks, Jesus!

THE DAYS THAT FOLLOWED

Today was beautiful. Mike was the first one to call this morning. He told me how glad he was I'm home, and told me he was having a party over at his house tomorrow night to welcome me back. I thanked him politely, but told him I didn't want any party. He was obviously upset. He asked me if he could come over to see me, I told him no. He said he still felt the same about me. I told him I didn't feel the same about him, and we should end it there. When he persisted, I told him I was committed to someone else. When he asked me who, I wouldn't tell him. I knew it was driving him crazy, but I gave him no satisfaction. I couldn't tell him anyway, Jesus. I tried not to enjoy the pleasure of seeing him squirm. Finally, he realized he was getting nowhere, so he agreed not to call again.

A lot of my friends came over and spent a good part of this morning. We had all kinds of things to talk about, and plans to make. Summer had just begun, so it was the perfect time to plan. Mom and Dad told me they had rented a place up in the Catskills, and I could invite my friends to come up and spend some time, but only a few at a time. That was great.

Tonight I went down to Gino's. Everybody was there. You would think they had seen a ghost, the way they looked at me when I walked in. But it didn't take long before we were our old selves again. It was like starting life all over again. Everything seemed new and fresh. I felt like a little kid.

I came home early, Jesus. I still get tired easily. I love looking up at you in that picture. It looks so real, just what I imagine you to be like. Good night, Jesus!

SECOND DAY

I just couldn't wait, Jesus. Today was so nice out, I called my friends and got the basketball out, and I tried to play. I was pathetic. I didn't play long and I didn't run at all. The doctor told me not to for a while. I couldn't anyway, it was too tiring. I had to spend the afternoon in bed. I was exhausted, but it was fun.

I don't know why Father Angelo doesn't call. He should be free; school is out. I miss him terribly. Good night.

THIRD DAY

Today was Sunday. I was surprised, Jesus, but everyone got up to go to church. I got up early to go to Mass by myself, and tried not to disturb anyone, thinking they would all sleep late, but, before long, everyone was up, so we all went together. Apparently, they had been going ever since I got sick.

But Mass was still boring, Jesus, though not as bad as it used to be. I went mostly because I wanted to receive Communion. The rest didn't really turn me on. Being there, I felt close to you. Putting up with the sermon and the rest is the least I can do in return for giving me back my health. And I'll still continue to go even if it is boring, as my way of saying, "thanks."

My mother invited Father Angelo over for dinner this afternoon. He came early, so we had time to talk. I asked him if he intended to drift away from me now that I was out of the hospital. He told me no. I asked how often I would see him. He said probably everyday in school. I didn't think it was funny. He apologized and said he doesn't really take it as lightly as it may seem.

At dinner we talked about all kinds of things; my father's work, and problems he was having with personnel, my brother and sister, the neighbors, what a good cook Mom was, about Father Angelo's work as a priest, and how he's the favorite topic of conversation around town. I told him it must be great to be so popular, and he said it complicates his life too much. He has no privacy.

Jesus, I've been so happy lately. I can't really believe I'm cured. The whole world seems new and full of life. I appreciate things I used to take for granted, and every little thing means so much more, like walking, and running, and

68

working in the garden. Today was a beautiful day. Thanks, Jesus. Good night!

LAZY SUMMER

Summer is going by so slowly, Jesus. I never thought I'd be looking forward to school, but I can't wait until September. I've been looking through college catalogues, trying to find a place I would like, and I got myself so "psyched up," I can't wait to finish high school, so I can get started on the things I really want to do. Father Angelo has been a big help, even though I haven't seen him much lately.

I took a walk out in the woods near the golf course today. It was so quiet and peaceful. There was a brook coursing through the woods and the water trickling over the rocks sounded like music. I saw all kinds of birds, Jesus; you sure do have some imagination to come up with so many different kinds of things. The air is so fresh and clean in the woods, and I feel so relaxed and happy. It's almost as if you are right nearby and I feel as if I'm part of you. I feel closer to you walking in the woods and talking to you as a friend, than I do going to church. I'm glad I finally found you, Jesus. You have really changed my life. As active as I used to be, and as involved as I was, there was always something missing, and when I was alone, I was so bored. But, ever since we have become friends, Jesus, life has become such an adventure, and the future so filled with endless possibilities, that I can't wait to get started on the work I really want to do. Good night!

OLD DREAMS-NEW HOPES

Summer finally ended, Jesus. The first days back to

school were fun. Everybody compared stories and we made plans for the year. Classes have already been going on for almost a month. This year it's fun, partly because everything we do is for the last time, but also because the courses are interesting.

I already applied to a number of colleges. I know it was early, but I have a very good record, and I also knew I could count on the doctors in the hospital to give me a good recommendation. They wrote beautiful letters, so did Father Angelo, and a few of my other teachers.

I got a wonderful letter back from the admissions director of one of the colleges, telling me they were very happy to accept me. It wasn't just a form letter, but a personal one. She said she was looking forward to meeting me, and knew I would enjoy their school. The college also has a medical school and a famous research hospital. Everything seemed to fit into place perfectly.

I see Father Angelo in class practically every day, Jesus. When I look up at him teaching, I can't help but think of you. Everything about him reminds me of you, and I'm so glad that he's part of my life. I don't know what the future will bring, but I hope we will always be as close as we are now. It will be so beautiful being able to work with him in the future.